WHEN MOOSE WAS YOUNG

JIM LATIMER

PICTURES BY

DONALD CARRICK

CHARLES SCRIBNER'S SONS • NEW YORK

The Crab Apple Woods

Moose grew up in Moosewood, a place of striped maple trees, with a blue-berry marsh, a Post Office, and an Animal Store. Moosewood was bordered by crab apples and broccoli, and on one side by a county road. When Moose was young his favorite place was The Store. The storekeepers, Newt and Frog, were purveyors of Deer brand doughnuts and Blue Jay jam—and fresh, fried potato chips. Frog fried the potato chips. Newt baked pretzels from stone-ground flour. In the spring Newt and Frog made elm syrup, and maple, and in the fall Frog made a pale pear butter. But most of all Moose liked Newt's beer—Newt's dark root beer, made from springwater and sassafras.

Once, in late summer, Moose walked to the Animal Store, his mind filled with visions of Newt's root beer. Inside the store, Newt was pacing. Frog looked worried.

"What's the matter?" Moose asked them.

"Skunk is gone," Newt answered.

Gone. Moose's eyes grew wide.

"Gone to look for crab apples," Frog explained. "For cider," he said. "Gone through the Broccoli Forest."

The Broccoli Forest. Moose shuddered. The Crab Apple Woods, a place of wild apple trees, was edged, almost engulfed, by a forest of tall broccoli, of pale shade and bumblebees—and wild boars. Moose had never been to the Broccoli Forest. No one from Moosewood ever went there as far as he knew. Not even Troll.

"But aren't crab apples sour?" Moose asked.

Frog nodded. "Skunk wants to make a new cider," he said. "Sour."

Moose blinked at him. He was not afraid of broccoli or wild boars. He was a *little* afraid of boars, and he was afraid of bumblebees, but he said to Newt and Frog, "I will go and look for Skunk."

Newt and Frog stood framed in their front doorway, watching Moose as he headed toward the broccoli.

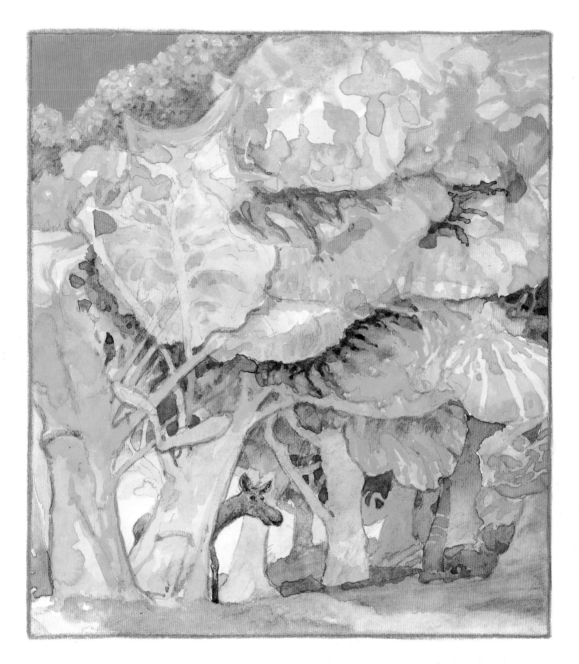

Moose walked through Moosewood to its farthest edge. A forest of pale stems crowned with dark flowers stood before him. He looked in. An eerie light filtered through the crown of broccoli. Everywhere there was a threatening, thrumming sound. Bumblebees, Moose thought. He shivered and stepped in.

Inside, the thrumming sound grew stronger. The green broccoli shade was denser and paler. Dark birds seemed to leap from the broccoli stems and disappear into the thrumming gloom. Moose took another step. Then another. He took seven steps altogether. Then, from behind the broccoli stems, there appeared suddenly one hundred wild boars. Moose was surrounded.

The biggest boar lowered its head and shook its huge toothed snout. Ninety-nine more boars shook their snouts. The big boar pawed the forest floor with its hoof. Ninety-nine more boars pawed the floor. Moose guessed what this meant. One hundred wild boars were going to charge him. The thrumming sound was almost deafening now. But Moose was not afraid— not *too* afraid.

"I do not want any broccoli," he told the boars. "I will not hurt your bees or dark birds," he said. "I am looking for Skunk."

Moose lowered his head, bracing himself for a charge, but at the mention of Skunk, the big boar suddenly stopped pawing. A startled, almost frightened expression came over him. He stared at Moose. The ninety-nine boars stared. The thrumming bees grew quiet. Then the one hundred wild boars all lifted their hooves and pointed to the left, in the direction of the Crab Apple Woods, showing the way Skunk had taken.

Moose was enormously puzzled by this, but he thanked the boars and took the leftward way.

Now the bumblebees and the dark birds were quiet, though Moose thought he felt them following him. He walked a long way through the broccoli gloom until at last the green stems parted and he looked out over a wild orchard crowded with low-branching, sharp-scented trees. It was the Crab Apple Woods.

Moose stood a moment, his ears alert. The woods were so still he could almost hear the sound of crab apples falling on the grass. But there was no sign or sound of Skunk. Moose rotated his ears. He lowered his head, searching for her scent. And then he saw her.

Skunk was lying on her back a short way ahead—lying still, with her eyes closed (though her nose was quivering).

Moose, alarmed, shouted, "Skunk!"

Skunk lifted her head. "What?" she answered.

"Are you all right?" Moose asked her.

"Perfect," she told him. "I am collecting crab apples. I have enough for a gallon." Skunk pointed to a cloth bag overflowing with apples.

"But," Moose asked her, "you weren't afraid?"

"Afraid of crab apples?"

"Of boars. Or dark birds—or bumblebees."

"Boars are afraid of skunks," Skunk told Moose. "And sometimes we *eat* bumblebees." Moose blinked at her. "*I* don't," she added. "But some skunks do."

Moose took a long look at Skunk. What a gritty, sturdy friend she was. He lifted her bag with his teeth and swung it over his shoulder. Moose and Skunk walked back to the Animal Store together—around the Broccoli Forest.

When they got back, Newt and Frog were standing, waiting in their doorway. Moose emptied Skunk's crab apples into the press around back, and Newt and Frog pressed them—into pulp and cider. One gallon.

Moose had never tried cider, sweet or sour. Newt and Frog said no one they knew had ever tried sour, but they tried it now. Moose tried it. It tasted—sour.

"It tastes sour," Moose told Skunk. "Dangerous," he added, thinking of the dark birds and bumblebees. Newt and Frog nodded.

The next day Skunk's Dangerous Sour Cider appeared in the window of the Animal Store.

"Dangerous cider?" Moose's mother asked him.

"Because collecting apples is dangerous," he told her.

Moose brought a sample of Skunk's cider to his mother and some to Crow and Bear, going His Moose Way Home.

Porcupine Comes Home

Once, when Moose was very young, he passed by Pigeon's tree. Crow, Pigeon's friend, was there. Porcupine was there, too, sitting in Pigeon's nest. Porcupine would not go away. Crow and Pigeon were standing nearby, staring at him. For a long time the birds stared at Porcupine in silence until Pigeon, without moving her eyes, leaned toward Crow.

"Tell him to go away," she whispered.

Crow tilted his head. "Porcupine," he said, "go away."

Porcupine did not go away. He sat in Pigeon's nest, looking sleek and satisfied. Porcupine closed his eyes, then opened them.

"Tell him again," Pigeon whispered, leaning toward Crow.

"GO AWAY," said Crow.

Porcupine did not go away.

"Tell him," Pigeon whispered, "that if he does not go away, I and all the pigeons in the world will be angry."

Crow said this.

Slowly, the heavy porcupine climbed out of Pigeon's nest. Slowly, he climbed down from Pigeon's tree, to the place where Moose was standing. Porcupine looked at Moose, then climbed back up again. Porcupine climbed into Pigeon's nest again and sat down heavily. He looked sleek and fat. Fat and sleek and comfortable.

Pigeon looked at Crow. She sighed a sigh of exasperation. "Ask young Moose if *he* can think of something," she whispered.

Crow asked Moose.

Moose circled Pigeon's tree unsteadily, staring up at Porcupine, trying to think. Moose circled Pigeon's tree again. He circled Pigeon's tree a third time.

"I can't think of anything," Moose told Crow.

So Porcupine stayed. And for many days afterward, until Moose was almost grown, he watched Pigeon and Porcupine becoming friends.

Once, when Moose was grown, already a hill on hoofs and thin stork legs, he passed by Pigeon's tree. Crow, Pigeon's friend, was there. So were Squirrel and Duck—and Gull and Rat and Wren. And Porcupine.

"We're making Porcupine an Honorary Squirrel," Squirrel told Moose.

"And a Bird for Life," explained Wren.

"Because Porcupine nests better than any bird," Pigeon explained.

"Better than a squirrel," said Squirrel.

"Because Hawk and Owl do *not* come when Porcupine is here," Rat explained.

Porcupine was sitting in Pigeon's nest, looking satisfied. Satisfied and comfortable.

Moose helped make Porcupine an Honorary Squirrel, and a Bird for Life, going His Moose Way Home.

Turkeys

On his way home Moose passed a group of wild turkeys. The turkeys, partly hidden in a thicket of nettles and skunk cabbage, were dressed in collars and black ties—with buckled, broad-brimmed hats. They were huddled together, whispering and murmuring. The turkeys were . . . Moose narrowed his eyes. A committee? A meeting? He stared at their starched collars and crossed black ties. They were *pilgrims*—turkeys dressed as pilgrims, and singing now. They were a congregation of pilgrim turkeys in broad hats and buckles, singing hymns together. And now they began to move.

The turkeys spread their wings, forming a wide circle. They began to hop. They hopped and skipped in rhythm. They flapped their wings, skipping and turning in place. Then they started to somersault. Moose gave himself a nip to see whether he might be dreaming.

But he wasn't. A group of wild turkeys *were* flapping, hopping, and somersaulting before him.

"What are you doing?" Moose called out suddenly.

Instantly the pilgrim turkeys were quiet. Blushing together, looking very embarrassed, they turned toward him, huddling close.

"What are *you* doing?" they asked. "Spying? Interfering where you have no business? Busybody," they said.

Moose apologized.

"Well, we're celebrating," the turkeys told him.

"Celebrating Thanksgiving," one added.

Moose's eyes widened. "But it's April," he said.

"Yes," the turkeys told him. "We celebrate Thanksgiving in April. And August. And June. Every month, every Thursday."

This was a Thursday, the last Thursday in April. "Oh," Moose said, "I see," though he didn't really.

"You don't really," one of the turkeys told him. "Thanksgiving is our special day," she said. "It's our ONLY special day. The only day WE are special," she explained to Moose. "Every other day we are *turkeys*."

"*Turkeys,*" said a rude rat who was passing.

"*Turkeys,*" said a snail.

"You see what I mean?" said the turkey.

Moose saw.

A group of grasshoppers were passing by. "*Turkeys,*" they called out.

"So we celebrate Thanksgiving every Thursday," the turkey resumed. "Sometimes we are Plymouth Pilgrims. We sing hymns. Sometimes we do a tribal dance, decked in feathers—or flowers."

"Sometimes we just cut loose," another turkey told Moose. "We have to," he said, "because no one likes a *turkey*. No one hops or somersaults with turkeys. No one ever gives a flower to a turkey."

Moose thought about all of this. He thought about Skunk on Valentine's Day. No one had wanted Skunk for a valentine. No one had ever given her a flower until once *he* had. But Moose had never given a flower to a turkey.

"Just wait," he said, and galloped away.

A short time later Moose returned with Skunk, with daffodils for the turkeys, and they somersaulted and celebrated together. Moose and Skunk cut loose with a group of wild turkeys, the last Thursday in April, going Their Moose Way Home.

Fox's Dream

"Wake up," Skunk whispered.

It was early. The woods were pale, filled with a clinging fog. Moose shivered. He did not wake up.

"Moose," Skunk whispered.

Moose made a wruffling sound. He opened his eyes, then closed them. Skunk pinched him.

"What?" he blurted, blinking awake. Moose stared into the eyes of his friend. "What?" he asked her.

"Fox had a dream," Skunk told him, whispering.

Moose stared at her. His coat was wet with fog and there was fog in his nose and ears.

"Fox traveled," Skunk continued, "in his dream, to the end of the county road." She paused. "And we are going to go there now," Skunk said. "Newt and Frog and Fox and Crow and Bear. And you."

The end of the county road. Moose tried to picture it. When he was very young he had stood beside the county road, watching for cars and trucks—watching for license plates. But no car or truck had come to the county road for a long time, and no one Moose knew had ever followed it beyond the borders of Moosewood. He could not guess where it led.

"They're waiting," Skunk whispered. "Newt and Frog and Fox and Crow and Bear. Let's go."

Moose went.

In the pale dawn, they found Fox waiting beside the county road, and with him Newt and Frog and Bear and Crow. Under a lowering sky they set out, seven animals, with Fox in front and Bear beside him, with Newt and Frog riding in Bear's ruff, and behind them Moose and Skunk and Crow— seven animals together, to the end of the county road.

Fox's company had walked a long way. Moosewood, now far behind, had given way to fields of gray thorns and broom straw. All day the seven animals had walked through watery sunshine, wondering what lay beyond each bend and rise in the road.

"Skunk," Moose whispered.

Skunk looked up at him.

"What was Fox's dream?" he asked her.

"We weren't going to tell you," she said.

Skunk looked at Crow, who was perched in Moose's antlers.

Crow inclined his head. "Let's tell him," he said.

Skunk nodded. "In Fox's dream there was a bright birch woods," she began, "and there were reindeer." Skunk paused. "Scary reindeer. And buffalos and pigeons."

Moose blinked.

"And there was a wonderful thing," Skunk continued. "A machine with carved animals. Animals that moved to music."

"And you could ride them," Crow told Moose.

Moose tried to imagine a machine with animals that moved to music—animals you could ride.

"We are hoping Fox made up the buffalos and the scary reindeer," Skunk said. Fox often made things up. "But," Skunk said, "we think the machine in Fox's dream is real."

Moose thought this over. Fox's head was filled with dreams and wishes. Lies, Armadillo called them. But Fox couldn't help it. His dreams were real to him. Probably, Moose thought, the end of the county road, the buffalo and reindeer, were not real. And yet, a machine that moved to music, with carved animals you could ride . . . Moose caught Crow's eye. He looked at Skunk.

"I think Fox's *machine* is real," he told them. "It *could* be real."

But by the end of their second day from Moosewood, the seven animals had seen no sign of pigeons or reindeer, no sign of buffalos or machines. Fox dreamed—he daydreamed—hard, but he could not make the things from his night dream come back, and by their third day from home Bear began to grow restless. He would be hibernating soon. He needed to get fat for fall. Newt and Frog had to do inventory at the Animal Store, and Crow had a lot of crow's work to do. Together they wished Fox good luck and good-bye and turned home.

"We will try again—sometime," said Newt.

Fox looked terrible. He looked at Skunk and Moose. "Do you have to go?" he asked them.

Moose shook his head.

"We're not too busy," Skunk said. "Let's keep going."

Fox brightened a little. As he walked, he flattened his ears, knitted his brows, and dreamed. Fox dreamed very hard. He dreamed all day. He dreamed until the wonderful machine came back into his mind, and he did not stop dreaming until Skunk and Moose could see it, too.

Moose caught his breath. Skunk caught hers. In Fox's dream they saw a ring of wooden animals, belled and tasseled and proud. There were a saddled bear with huge carved buckles and a rabbit decorated with cherubs. And there were a leaping frog and a camel. Moose saw a rampant lion and a tiger in flowing drapery, and a jeweled, tasseled reindeer. There were a carved stork and a crane, an elephant and a zebra, a rooster—and horses. There were horses of every color and breed, decorated with carved moons and ribbons, with fish scales and demons and flowers. And as the three animals watched, awed, the machine began to move.

The stork and crane seemed to take flight. Behind them came the elephant and the camel and then a seahorse Moose had not noticed before. Then came a pair of pigs and a pair of rabbits. Fox, in a dreamy voice, whispered, "Hurry" and boarded the machine. Moose and Skunk clambered up behind him.

The three animals stood a moment on the moving platform. Fox found a horse to ride. Moose straddled an elephant, his chin resting on its head, his hooves almost touching the floor. Skunk, beside him, scrambled onto a stork. Above them wooden rods swept out from a pole like the spokes of an umbrella. Moose sighed. Bells were ringing. Beside him Skunk began to rise and fall in rhythm, and almost before Moose knew it the floor of the machine was turning fast. He saw Skunk and Fox leaning and felt himself leaning, banking outward, rising and falling on his elephant. And then the trees nearby began to blur.

Moose closed his eyes, then opened them. It was like moving through a sideways rain; like sleighing, wild and free. It was like flying. Moose closed his eyes again and for a long time he plunged and soared—and flew.

When he opened his eyes the machine had slowed. The bells were almost still.

"Skunk," he whispered.

"What?" Skunk answered. She opened her eyes and looked at her friend.

"I felt like . . ." Moose groped. "Like an elephant, an elephant flying."

Skunk nodded. "Me, too," she said. "Like a stork and an elephant." Fox had felt like a stork and a horse and an elephant.

Together, Moose and Skunk and Fox had taken flight in Fox's dream—on Fox's *carousel*—going Their Moose Way Home.

JIM LATIMER, a graduate of the Bank Street College of Education and Ohio State University, has taught in nursery school and in several universities. His work has been published in magazines and in anthologies. His first book for children, *Going the Moose Way Home*, illustrated by Donald Carrick, was published in 1988. Mr. Latimer received the 1988–89 Minnesota Book Award in the children's book category for *Going the Moose Way Home*.

DONALD CARRICK illustrated more than eighty books, many of them written by his wife, Carol Carrick. Two of the books he illustrated, *Bear Mouse,* by Berniece Freschet, and *Doctor Change,* by Joanna Cole, received the Irma Simonton Black Award of the Bank Street College of Education. Donald and Carol Carrick were awarded the 1988–89 California Young Readers Medal for *What Happened to Patrick's Dinosaurs?* Donald Carrick died in 1989 at his home in Edgartown, Massachusetts.

PUBLISHER'S NOTE

The illustrations for this book were close to completion at the time of Donald Carrick's death. The jacket and the pictures he was unable to finish—those on pages 10, 28, 29, 30, and 31— were rendered by Rae Ecklund from Mr. Carrick's detailed color sketches.